Are
you
quite
polite
?

Margaret K. McElderry Books * An imprint of Simon & Schuster Children's Publishing Division * 1230 Avenue of the Americas, New York, New York 10020 * Text copyright © 2006 by Alan Katz * Illustrations copyright © 2006 by David Catrow * All rights reserved, including the right of reproduction in whole or in part in any form. * Book design by Sonia Chaghatzbanian * The text for this book is set in Kosmik. * The illustrations are rendered in watercolors, colored pencil, and ink. * Manufactured in China * 10 9 8 7 6 5 4 3 2 1 * Library of Congress Cataloging-in-Publication Data * Katz, Alan. * Are you quite polite? : silly dilly manners songs / Alan Katz and David Catrow.— 1st ed. * p. cm. * Summary: Presents humorous lyrics to such familiar children's songs as "Pop Goes the Weasel," "Twinkle, Twinkle, Little Star," and "Hey Diddle Diddle." * ISBN-13: 978-0-689-86970-9 * ISBN-10: 0-689-86970-3 (hardcover) * 1. Children's songs—United States—Texts. 2. Humorous songs—Texts.[1. Humorous songs. 2. Songs.] I. Title: Are you quite polite? II. Catrow, David, ill. III. Title. * PZ8.3.K1275Do 2006 * 782.42—dc22   2005001124

FIRST
EDITION

To Stacey and Jacob, two of the best (and best-mannered) kids in the whole wide world—A. K.

To Mom and Dad,
all silliness aside—D. C.

Are you quite polite?

silly dilly
manners
songs

Alan Katz

David Catrow

Margaret K. McElderry Books • New York London Toronto Sydney

Drinkin' at the Fountain

(To the tune of "Polly Wolly Doodle")

Oh, don't put your mouth
On the waterspout
When you're drinkin' at the fountain every day
Your breath's like trout
We can do without,
And your tongue is a wormy germ buffet!

What a smell
I'm not well
So I'll yell, "Please get away!"
And from now on I am trusting
That you won't be so disgusting
(And stop drinkin' from the toilet, by the way!)

Jimmy Picks Boogers

(To the tune of "The Blue-Tail Fly")

My friend Jim has a mouth that lies
A little south of his bright eyes
And in between, of course, a nose
That's where his index finger goes!

Jimmy picks boogers day and night
Jimmy picks boogers, what a sight
Jimmy picks boogers, it's not right
He just flicks them away!

It is a habit hard to break
His finger travels like a snake
If this keeps up, one day I fear
He'll tunnel right up through his ear!

Jimmy picks boogers—listen, chum
Picking your nose is really dumb
Though it's good to have a green thumb,
Don't get yours Jimmy's way!

The Dirty Song

(To the tune of "Red River Valley")

Oh, your shoes and your socks are all muddy
'Cause you hopped and went plop in the slop
So before you go inside, my buddy,
Wipe your feet or get stopped with a mop!

And you might ask Mom to beg your pardon
From the smell you can tell she's surprised
'Cause the tug-of-war was in her garden,
Which you didn't know was fertilized!

There's a truckload of soil in the bathroom
From the dirt on the shirt you heave-ho'd
What a mess! Better go grab the vacuum!
Or come spring, right there flowers might grow!

Oh, it's fun to get messy and mucky
You'll find grime all the time when you roam
When you slide into third, you'll get yucky
So please clean up before you head home!

Pop Separates Them!

(To the tune of "Pop Goes the Weasel!")

Mark and Sue are brother and sis,
But Sue says that she hates him
Mark tells Sue, "Go live in a cave!"
Pop separates them!

Mark says she stinks
Sue breaks his stuff
And always aggravates him
He taunts her
She pinches back
Pop separates them!

Mark and Sue just can't get along
It's wild how she baits him
They scream and snarl and threaten and yell
Pop separates them!

So if you've got a bro or a sis,
Be friendly, if not kissy
Don't fight like Mark and Sue because
Their pop's too busy!

Don't Chew Gum in the Classroom

(To the tune of "Take Me Out to the Ball Game")

Don't chew gum in the classroom
Don't chew gum while in church
A kid I know chewed in the barber chair
Soon he had gum where he used to have hair
So don't chew, chew, chew on the choo-choo
Don't chomp, chomp when meeting with scouts
There's no merit badge when your teeth
All rot and drop out!

While we're talking 'bout chewing,
While we're thinking 'bout gum,
Dispose of yours properly, wrapped and neat
Don't stick it under a table or seat
And don't spit your wad on the sidewalk
Be kind when gum chewing's through
I enjoy a piece now and then
But not on my shoe!

You're Invited!

(To the tune of "The Muffin Man")

When you're a birthday party guest,
Don't smear ice cream
On your friend's vest
Or hide his shoes in the ice chest
They'll freeze and he'll complain.

When at a birthday party bash
Don't throw the presents
In the trash,
And googly eyes when cameras flash
Just do not entertain.

Another thing you shouldn't do
Is give a kid
A cake shampoo
You'd get a laugh, but also you'd
Get frosting on his brain.

Just keep food items
Off of clothes
No candies in
Your ears or nose
Try to go home with all ten toes
They'll have you back again!

Rules, Rules, Rules

(To the tune of "The Mexican Hat Dance")

Don't hit
Don't run
Don't spit
Not even
A cherry pit
Don't call your friend "nitwit,"
And try not to throw a fit!

Oh . . .
Respect everyone in your family
Don't roar like a lion, act lamb-ly
Just at throat checkups stick out your tongue!

Don't whine
Don't cry
Don't moan
You'll sound like
A dial tone
When in a trouble zone
Don't blame it all on your clone!

Oh . . .
Don't shove anyone when you're playing
When in the hallways do not run
In other words, here's what I'm saying:
Be a kid, but don't have any fun!

Writing Thank-Yous

(To the tune of "Alouette")

Writing thank-yous
Really is important
Mom says thank-yous
Show your gratitude.

Kate gave me a pair of skates
I use them as paperweights
They're too small
Still I'll scrawl
Tha-a-ank you . . .

Writing thank-yous
Is still what I must do,
Though my party
Was in two thousand two.

I'll write thanks to my pal Paul
He gave me a basketball
Won't inflate
Still I'll state
Tha-a-ank you . . .

Writing thank-yous
Really is exhausting
Hand is cramping
Fingers all are numb.

Though I'm slow, I'm plodding through
Only have ten notes to do
Love the skates
Paul—ball's great
Eight more cards
This is hard
Oh-oh-oh-oh . . .

Mom, if you would
Let me skip my thank-yous,
I would write a
Thank-you note to you!

Peter the Sneezer

(To the tune of "The Man on the Flying Trapeze")

When Pete goes, "Ah-choo,"
Everybody yells, "Freeze!"
There's no superglue
Stick-i-er than his sneeze
The worst part is, he always sneezes in threes
No wonder the town moved away!

He sneezed down a statue,
Whooshed leaves off of trees,
Blew out all the locks
In the Florida Keys
The people all went to him on bended knees
(They couldn't stand up anyway!)

They said to him, "Peter,
Each time that you sneeze
You seem to whip up
A tornado-force breeze,
And so we are asking and begging you, please
You must cover up when you spray!"

So Peter, he covered
Next time he ah-chooed
'Cause though he was sneezy,
He was a cool dude
And sneezing without cov-er-ing is just rude
The townsfolk moved back that same day!

Don't Talk with Beans in Your Mouth

(To the tune of "Michael, Row the Boat Ashore")

Don't talk with beans in your mouth
It's bad man-ners
Don't talk with beans in your mouth
Or banan-ners!

If you stuff cheese in your cheek,
Don't sing opera
Folks you're eating with'll freak
And they'll stop ya!

Talking with cake in your jaw
Is just not good
If you say, "Mm, I wan mowr,"
It's not un-der-stood.

If you've stories to reveal
Though you're busting,
Chew and swallow your oatmeal
Or you're dis-gust-ing.

With bologna in your face
Don't do Shakespeare
You will be a big disgrace
That's the breaks, dear!

Try Being Neat

(To the tune of "America the Beautiful")

Look in your room
Is it a mess
'Cause cleaning's what you dread?
And does it take a
Bulldozer
For you to find your bed?

Try being neat
It's quite a treat,
And the best news is this:
Under that clump
Of clothes, that lump
Could be your baby sis!

Check your backpack
For last week's snack
It's prob'ly hiding there
Don't touch it, though
Because you know
Pudding should not have hair!

Try being neat
It's quite a feat
It's good to show you care
So organize
Al-pha-bet-ize
All of your underwear!

Are You Quite Polite?

(To the tune of "Do Your Ears Hang Low?")

Are you quite polite
Having dinner every night?
Do you stomp up to the table
And then chomp in monster bites?
Are you eating or just slurping?
And do you conclude by burping?
Are you quite polite?

Do you utter "please"
When you'd like to have some peas?
Are your elbows on the table?
(Or your ankles? Or your knees?)
Do you use the right utensil?
Or eat pasta with a pencil?
Are you quite polite?

And what is the chance
There's a napkin on your pants?
Do you make so many crumbs,
Your seat is popular with ants?
Do you finish and then dash,
Leaving dishes and the trash?
You, I won't invite!

Quiet in the Library

(To the tune of "Twinkle, Twinkle, Little Star")

When you're in the library,
Quiet is the way to be
Please talk softly
Make the choice
Only use your indoor voice
Libraries are full of joys,
But they can't be full of noise!

Someone is a bit too loud
We don't need a one-kid crowd
I won't beat
Round the bush
Please be still
Won't you shoosh?
I will have to ring this bell,
And I'm gonna start to YELL!

**NOW I'M SCREAMING
NOISE MUST CEASE!
WE ALL WANT TO WORK IN PEACE!
SILENCE NOW
LET'S BE CALM
DON'T MAKE ME
TELL YOUR MOM
QUIET IN THE LIBRARY!!!**
OOPS, THE NOISY ONE IS . . . me.

The Late Song

(To the tune of "Hey Diddle Diddle")

If you want greatness,
Be careful of lateness
'Cause being tardy is gross
To keep friendships thriving
Do not be arriving
When they're set to say "adios"!

Take my friend Artie,
Who came to my party,
Though I would say he was late
Showed up June 11
Yelled, "Yay, you are seven!"
I said, "No, May 1st
I turned eight!"

Then there is Ingrid,
Who did a bad thingrid
We said we'd meet in swim clothes
But while I was waiting,
The lake froze for skating
What took her so long?
No one knows.

I'm saying rhyme-ly
That "Always be timely"
Is something you oughta know
Oops, have to meet Shirley,
And she's always early
Don't wanna be late—gotta go!

BUS
STOP

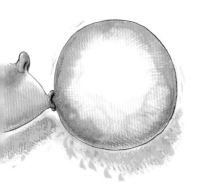